Franklin Plays the Game

Franklin

Kids Can Press acknowledges the financial support of the Ontario Arts Council, the Canada Council for the Arts and the Government of Canada, through the CBF, for our publishing activity.

Published in Canada by
Kids Can Press Ltd.
25 Dockside Drive
Toronto, ON M5A 0B5

Published in Canada by
Kids Can Press Ltd.
2250 Military Road
Tonawanda, NY 14150

www.kidscanpress.com

The hardcover edition of this book is smyth sewn casebound.
The paperback edition of this book is limp sewn with a drawn-on cover.
Manufactured in Buji, Shenzhen, China, in 7/2015 by WKT Company

CM 95 0 9 8 7 6
CDN PA 95 20 19 18 17 16 15 14 13 12 11
CMC PA 13 0 9 8 7 6 5 4 3 2

Library and Archives Canada Cataloguing in Publication

Bourgeois, Paulette
     Franklin plays the game / written by Paulette Bourgeois ;
illustrated by Brenda Clark.

(A classic Franklin story)
ISBN 978-1-894786-99-7

     1. Franklin (Fictitious character : Bourgeois) – Juvenile fiction.
I. Clark, Brenda II. Title. III. Series: Classic Franklin story

PS8553.O85477F78 2013   jC813'.54   C2012-907878-6

Kids Can Press is a lorus™ Entertainment company

Franklin Plays the Game

Written by Paulette Bourgeois
Illustrated by Brenda Clark

Kids Can Press

FRANKLIN could slide down a riverbank. He could tie his shoes and count by twos. He could walk to Bear's house all by himself. But Franklin couldn't kick a soccer ball straight. That was a problem because Franklin wanted to be the best player on his team.

Franklin loved soccer. He liked the running and the dribbling. He especially liked the uniforms. He wore his purple and yellow jersey and matching shin pads, even when he wasn't playing soccer.

Sometimes he slept with his soccer ball and dreamed of scoring goals.

Before every game, Franklin practiced in the park. He kicked the ball with the inside of his foot again and again. He did warm-up stretches and cool-down walks.

Still, Franklin had trouble. He couldn't run very fast ... even without a soccer ball between his feet. And when Franklin kicked the ball, it never went where he intended.

Goose watched Franklin's ball fly into the bushes.

"I'll never score a goal," said Franklin sadly.

"Neither will I," said Goose. "I keep forgetting the rule that says I cannot use my wings unless I'm the goalkeeper. Everybody gets mad at me."

Goose showed Franklin how wide her wings stretched.

Beaver was watching, too.

"And I'll never score a goal," she said, "because my tail is so long and heavy that it drags me down."

She ran for a bit. Franklin and Goose could see the problem.

"No wonder we never win any games," grumbled Franklin.

It was true. Franklin's team had not won a game all season. Bear's team won every game.

Losing didn't bother Coach. She said the same thing before each game: "Let's have fun out there!"

Losing didn't bother Franklin's parents, who shouted "Nice try!" whenever Franklin got the ball.

But it bothered Franklin a lot.

What's wrong?" asked Franklin's father.

"I never score a goal," answered Franklin.

"But you try and you have fun," said Franklin's father. "That's the important thing."

Franklin nodded. That's what all the grown-ups said. But he really wanted everybody to cheer for him. He wanted to score a goal.

It wasn't only Franklin who felt that way. Each of Franklin's friends wanted to score a goal. But the harder they tried, the worse they played. Franklin forgot where to stand. Goose forgot what to do.

Whenever the ball came to Franklin's teammates, they rushed toward it. Players tripped over feet and tails and long ears. They crashed into a heap.

Coach helped untangle the players. "You have to work together as a team. You have to share the ball."

But it wasn't easy to do. Their team lost again.
It made the players feel sad. Franklin huddled inside
his shell. Beaver tucked in her tail and Goose folded
her wings.

The other team crossed the field to shake hands.

"Nice try," said Bear.
Franklin didn't come out of his shell.
Bear bounced the soccer ball up and down.
"Come on out, Franklin," said Bear.

Franklin poked out his head. At that moment,
Bear's ball was coming up. Franklin bounced the ball
off the top of his head. It went flying straight to Goose.
She spread her wings.
"Saved!" Franklin shouted.

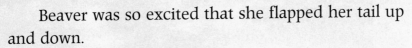

Beaver was so excited that she flapped her tail up and down.

"That's it!" cried Franklin.

"What's it?" asked Bear.

Franklin smiled at Beaver and Goose. "I think I know how we can score goals," he said, patting his head. "But it will take some teamwork."

Every day until the next game, Franklin and the team practiced in the park. Coach helped them work on a special play.

They giggled and laughed and dribbled and bounced.

They played in the rain and slid in the mud.

One day, Bear came by. "What are you doing?" he asked.

"Just having fun," said Franklin. He could hardly wait until the next game.

It was time for the final game. The teammates huddled together.

"Let's show them what we can do," said Franklin.

But within the first minutes of the game, Bear's team scored a goal.

"Team," said Coach, "it's time for your special play." Goose went into the goal. She used her wings as much as she wanted and made three spectacular saves. The crowd cheered.

Goose spotted Franklin on the field and tossed the ball to him. It landed on Franklin's head. One strong bob, and Franklin sent the ball soaring to Beaver. With a swish of her tail, Beaver passed the ball to Rabbit. He lifted his big foot and kicked the ball into the net. Franklin's team scored!

The teammates jumped for joy and hugged one another.

For the rest of the game, they played their best. Franklin even headed the ball twice, but nobody on his team scored again. Bear's team scored one more time to win the game.

Coach gave all her players a ribbon.

"You should be proud of yourselves," she said. "You worked hard as a team. You ALL helped score that goal."

Franklin's parents invited the team out for a treat.
"Why?" asked Franklin. "Our team didn't win."
"You look like winners to us," said his father.
Franklin had to agree. They were tired and dirty
and happy. Sure signs of a winning team.